SNUG AS A BUG?

 happy yak

For my lovely Mom! Thank you for always being there and for supporting my writing adventures x
K.N.

For Dara and Walter
A.W.

Brimming with creative inspiration, how-to projects, and useful information to enrich your everyday life, quarto.com is a favorite destination for those pursuing their interests and passions.

Inspiring | Educating | Creating | Entertaining

© 2023 Quarto Publishing Group USA Inc.
Text © 2023 Karl Newson
Illustrations © 2023 Alex Willmore

Karl Newson has asserted his right to be identified as the author of this work. Alex Willmore has asserted his right to be identified as the illustrator of this work.

First published in 2023 by Happy Yak, an imprint of The Quarto Group.
100 Cummings Center, Suite 265D
Beverly, MA 01915, USA.
T (978) 282-9590 F (978) 283-2742
www.quarto.com

A CIP record for this book is available from the Library of Congress.

ISBN: 978 0 7112 7486 0

9 8 7 6 5 4 3 2 1

Manufactured in Guangdong, China CC012023.

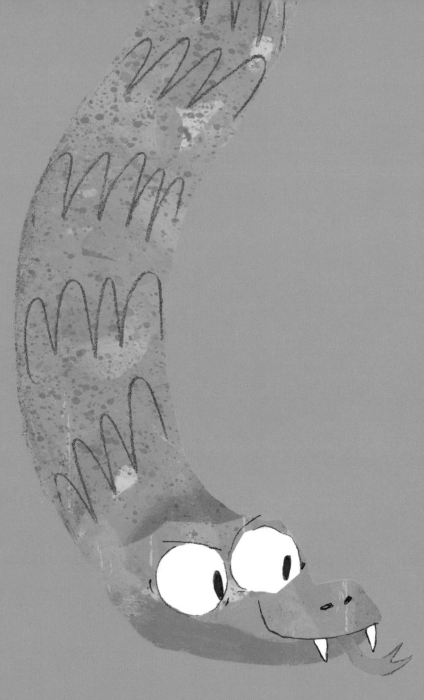

KARL
NEWSON

ALEX
WiLLMORE

SNUG AS A BUG?

happy yak

I'm as snug as a bug in a rug, I am.

As snug as a bug could be.

There has never been a bug
in **THE WHOLE WIDE WORLD**
so happily snug as me!

Why, **tasty** bug,
  it's only me...
      It's time for my dinner,
          you see.

But I've already *had* my dinner...

My, my, little bug,
aren't you a treat!
You're just in time
for a bite to eat...

No, thank you,
I've *already* eaten!

I'm as snug as a bug in a rug, I am.
As snug as a bug could be.
There has never been a bug
IN A CAVE OF
CERTAIN DEATH
so happily snug
as me!

I'm as snug as a bug in a rug, I am.
As snug as a bug could be.
There has never been a bug
IN A FOREST OF DOOM
so happily snug as me!

Aha!
Somewhere
safe
to rest
my legs
and catch
my breath
and...

WHY DOES THIS
KEEP HAPPENING
TO ME?

I'M AS SNUG AS A BUG IN A RUG, I AM!
AS SNUG AS A BUG COULD BE.
THERE HAS NEVER BEEN A BUG
FLYING...
FALLING...
FLAPPING!
SO HAPPILY SNUG AS MEEEEE!

Why did I answer the door?

Greetings bug!
How nice of you to drop by!

Nice to eat you, too.
WHAT?!

Nice.   **Eat.**

To.   **You!**

Wait.

What's that sound?

OH FIDDLESTICKS!

There has never been a bug

IN A CROCODILE'S
BUBBLE-POPPING-REALLY-SMELLY BELLY
so happily snug as me.

I outran a
SLURPING SNAKE.

I escaped
A CAVE OF CERTAIN DEATH.

I trekked through
A FOREST OF DOOM.

I flew
ON THE BACK OF A BIRD.

I sailed a
LEAF OVER A WATERFALL.

And I am NOT snug here.
NOT AT ALL.

You ate the *wrong* bug!

I'M GOING HOME!

I'm as snug as a bug in a rug, I am.
As snug as a bug could—

DING-
DONG!

Nope.
GO BUG SOMEONE ELSE!
There has never been a bug
IN THE WHOLE WIDE WORLD
so happily snug as me.